CATCHING THOUGHTS

by **BONNIE CLARK**

illustrated by **SUMMER MACON**

beaming books
MINNEAPOLIS

For A, S, and A. And for you.
—B.C.

For Loren, Chris, and Sam.
—S.M.

Published in 2020 by Beaming Books, an imprint of 1517 Media. All rights reserved. No part of this book may be reproduced without the written permission of the publisher. Email copyright@1517.media. Printed in Canada.

26 25 24 23 22 21 20   1 2 3 4 5 6 7 8 9

Hardcover ISBN: 978-1-5064-6416-9
Ebook ISBN: 978-1-5064-6662-0

Library of Congress Cataloging-in-Publication Data

Names: Clark, Bonnie, 1979- author. | Macon, Summer, illustrator.
Title: Catching thoughts / by Bonnie Clark ; illustrated by Summer Macon.
Description: Minneapolis, MN : Beaming Books, 2020. | Audience: Ages 3-8. |
   Summary: "A child learns to acknowledge an unwanted thought, show it
   compassion, and then actively let it go so she can focus on positive
   thoughts instead"-- Provided by publisher.
Identifiers: LCCN 2019055359 (print) | LCCN 2019055360 (ebook) | ISBN
   9781506464169 (hardcover) | ISBN 9781506466620 (ebook)
Subjects: CYAC: Thoughts and thinking--Fiction. | Attitude (Psychology)
Classification: LCC PZ7.1.C574 Cat 2020 (print) | LCC PZ7.1.C574 (ebook)
   | DDC [E]--dc23
LC record available at https://lccn.loc.gov/2019055359
LC ebook record available at https://lccn.loc.gov/2019055360

VN0004589; 9781506464169; JUN2020

Beaming Books
510 Marquette Avenue
Minneapolis, MN 55402

I have this thought I don't like.
It showed up on a bad day.

At first
it was really no big deal . . .

just a teeny, tiny,
little thought.

But after a while,
the thought
followed me
everywhere I went.

It tripped me up when I wasn't expecting it.

I tried to unthink
my unwanted thought.
But that just made me
think about it more!

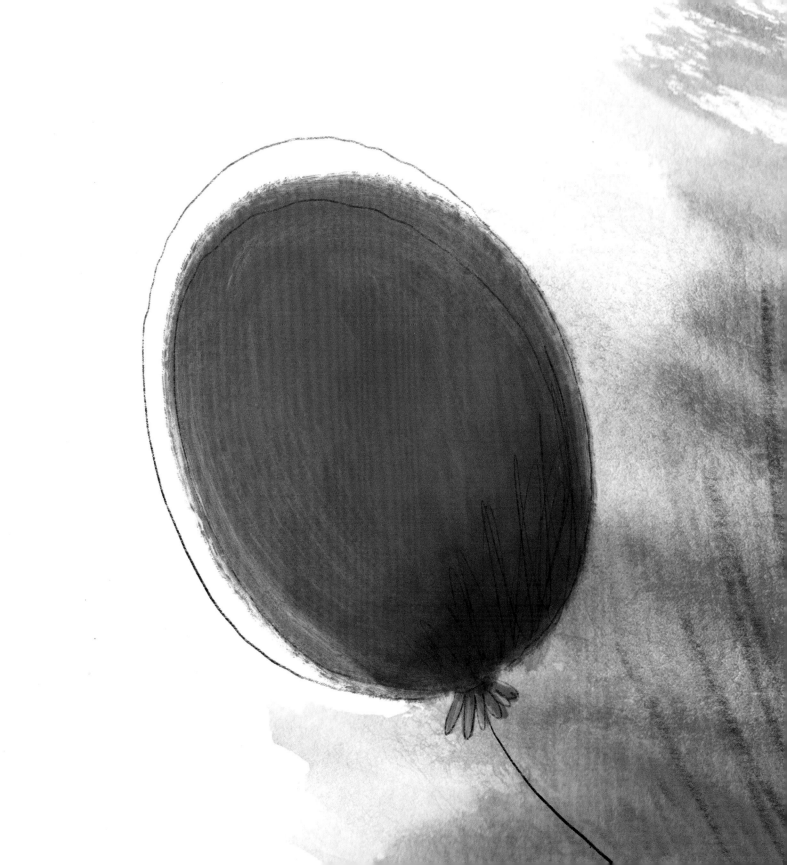

This thought made me angry,
so I yelled, "Get out of my brain!"

It stayed.

I sat down and cried.
It didn't care.

It seemed like there was no more room in my head
for anything but the one horrible thought.

I had to do something.

I took a deep breath and looked at it.
Maybe it wasn't so big.

I smiled and said:

That's when I noticed it.
It was small. But it was beautiful.

I reached up and caught it!

This beautiful thought gave me an idea . . .

I turned to that old thought and grinned.
"From now on, I'll be catching new thoughts!"

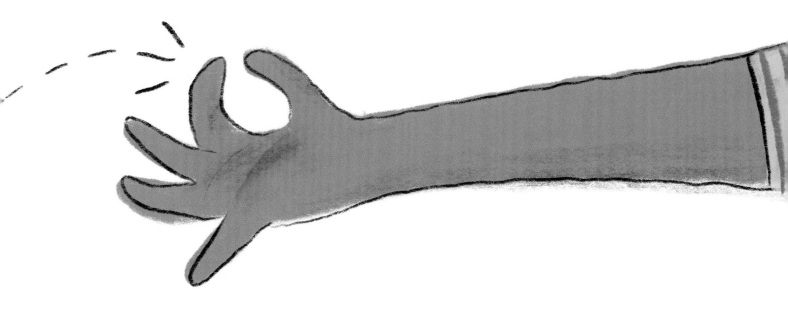

And then I gently pushed the old thought aside.

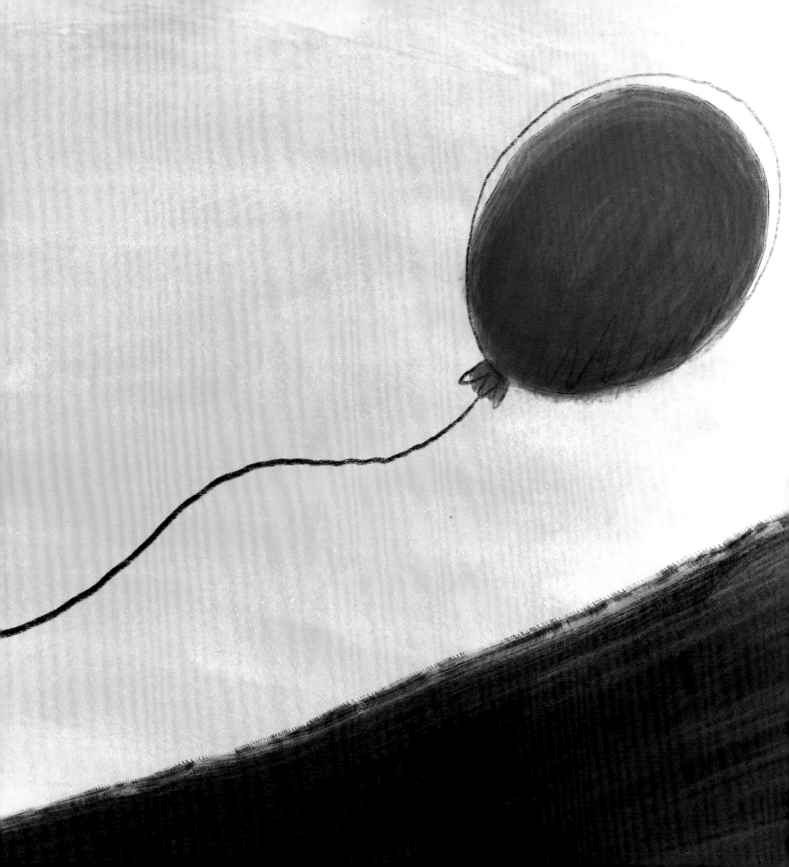

I grabbed on to thoughts
that were HOPEFUL,
    and gathered up thoughts
        that were LOVELY.

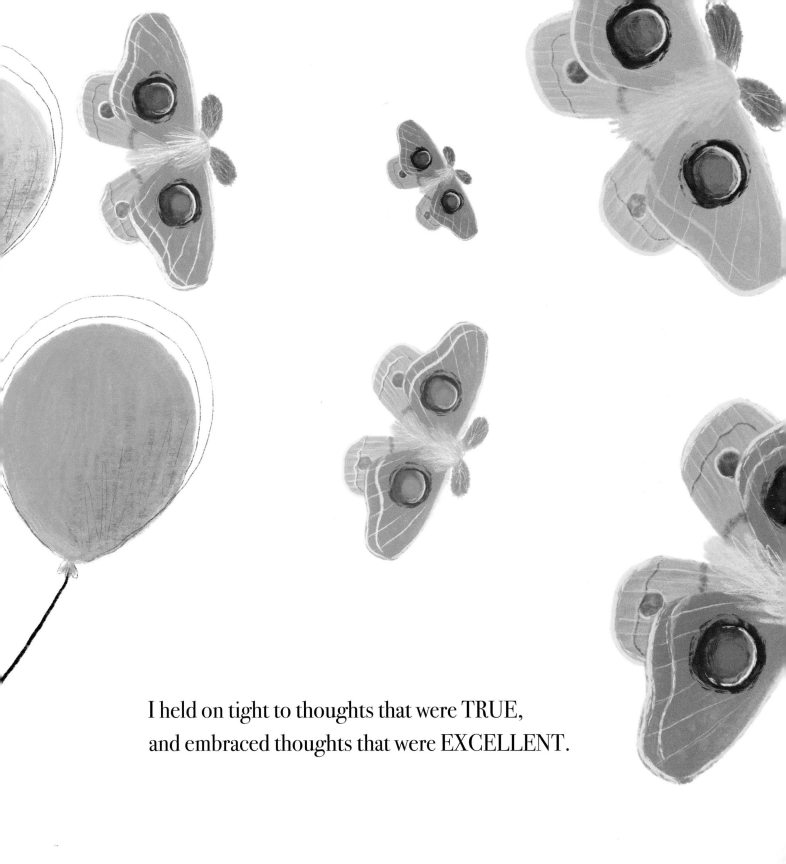

I held on tight to thoughts that were TRUE,
and embraced thoughts that were EXCELLENT.

I danced with
thoughts of pure JOY.

I collected thoughts
that were CLEAR and CALM.

I realized that the more
positive thoughts I caught,
the smaller that old,
negative thought became.

And whenever
that old thought
tries to come back into view. . .

. . . I can just say, "Hello,"
and politely ask it to leave . . .

. . . and fill my world with all the good
thoughts that I choose to put in my mind instead.

ABOUT THE AUTHOR AND ILLUSTRATOR

 **BONNIE CLARK** is a children's book author living in Canton, Georgia. She believes childhood is the most important time in a person's life. Bonnie lives with her husband, their children, and two French bulldogs.

 **SUMMER MACON** was raised in an itty-bitty town in southern New Mexico. In the summertime you can find her rock-climbing, paddle-boarding, mountain biking, or doodling on her contracts.